W9-CEM-567

Peepsqueak!

Written and illustrated by Leslie Ann Clark

HARPER

An Imprint of HarperCollinsPublishers

Library of Congress Cataloging-in-Publication Data is available.
ISBN 978-0-06-207801-8
Typography by Jeanne L. Hogle
12 13 14 15 16 SCP 10 9 8 7 6 5 4 3 2 1
❖
First Edition

To my Bear, with love.
To Bob and Ann forever!
To Nolan, Henry, and Isaac—kisses from YaYa!
To Juju, Em Em, Lolo, and the Crons!

—L.C.

One sunny morning, Peepsqueak popped out of his shell.
All the other baby chicks were stretching and yawning.
But not Peepsqueak! Because why?

He was on the move!

P.S.

Peepsqueak fluttered.

Peepsqueak hopped.

But more than anything, Peepsqueak wanted to fly . . . **HIGH!**

"Don't even try!" mooed Big Brown Cow.
"You can't fly high!"

But Peepsqueak did not listen. Because why?
He was on the move!

The big stone wall looked like the
perfect place to take off.

Peepsqueak jumped up, Up, UP!

And then he fell

down, Down,

DOWN

into the soft green grass.

"My oh my!" bleated Big Sheep. "You can't fly high!"

But Peepsqueak did not listen.
Because why?

He was on the move!

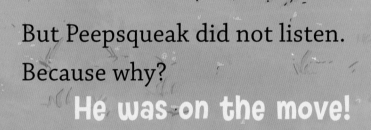

The nice round hill looked like the perfect place to take off.

Peepsqueak jumped up, Up, UP!

And then he fell

down,

Down,

DOWN into the soft green grass.

"You're a little guy," quacked Yellow Duck.
"You can't fly high!"

But Peepsqueak did not listen.
Because why?
He was on the move!

The tower of chicks
looked like the perfect
place to take off.
Peepsqueak jumped **up, Up, UP!**

And then he fell **down,**

Down,

DOWN into the soft green grass.

"Silly Peepsqueak!" squeaked Baby Bunny.
"Even if you try, you can't fly high!"

But Peepsqueak did not listen. Because why?
He was on the move!

The big rock looked like the perfect place to take off.
Peepsqueak jumped **up, Up, UP!**

nd then he fell

down,

Down,

DOWN into the soft green grass.

Peepsqueak jumped

and hopped

and flopped.

Peepsqueak tried to fly all day long!

He tried and tried,

but he could not fly high.
His momma gave him a
great big hug!

"Don't you cry, little guy," honked Old Gray Goose as he lifted Peepsqueak up.

Peepsqueak held on **tight, Tight, TIGHT** to Old Gray Goose and **up** they went!

Peepsqueak and Old Gray Goose flew **high, High, HIGH.**

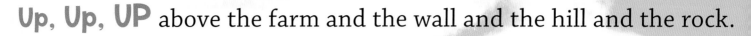

Up, Up, **UP** above the farm and the wall and the hill and the rock.

And then **down,**

Down,

DOWN into the soft green grass.

"You flew HIGH!" mooed Big Brown Cow.

"My oh my!" bleated Big Sheep.

"Up to the sky!" quacked Yellow Duck.

"You flew high!" squeaked Baby Bunny.

Peepsqueak was as happy as he could be!
Then he saw the pond, and he got another idea.

"**No,** Peepsqueak! You can't swim!"
shouted his friends.
But Peepsqueak did not listen. Because why?

He was on the move!